LARGE PRINT

Princess Stories

Brown Watson
ENGLAND

Princess Lalita's Wish

Lalita was a poor girl with no mother and father. She worked hard, did well at school, and tried to stay happy by dancing all the time. She skipped and twirled everywhere she went.

One day, she heard the townspeople talking about a dance competition. This is my chance! she thought. I shall enter and win, to show what I can do. Who knows, there may even be a prize!

Lalita danced her very best in the competition, and made it to the finals. A smart boy asked her to be his partner for the last dance. He took her hand and off they went. They seemed to float across the floor!

By the end of the dancing, Lalita was quite breathless. They waited nervously for the results. Lalita and her partner were the winners! "Congratulations!" said the boy. "My name is Mitali."

"Watch this!" Mitali whispered, and rubbed the trophy three times. With a whoosh, a magical flying carpet appeared! "This is your real prize," said Mitali. "It can grant three wishes. What do you wish for?"

"I wish that I lived in a fine house, with a real mum and dad – and with you as my friend," said Lalita. And with a twinkle of magic and a flash of light, Lalita's wishes were granted. Imagine what a happy dance she did then!

The Princess and the Pea

Things were getting tricky for
Prince Adam. He was supposed to be
marrying a princess, but he couldn't find
one he liked! They all seemed too silly,
or too vain, or too boring.

"Mother," he said one day.
"Am I looking for the wrong things in my wife? None of these people seems exactly right for a princess!" His mother hugged him and told him to wait and see what happened.

That night, a terrible storm blew up.
The prince lay in his bed, thinking about
princesses and listening to the thunder rage
and the winds blow. Then he heard a
knock at the castle door.

His parents were amazed to find
a young girl standing outside in the rain.
"Oh, please let me in!" she cried. "I am a
princess and have lost my royal guide.
I am so cold, and so tired!"

While the king gave the girl towels and dry clothes, the queen made up her bed for the night. First, she took a dried pea and put it on the bed. Then she piled the bed high with mattresses and blankets.

"This will put her to the test!" smiled the queen. "If she is a true princess, she will be so sensitive that she will never sleep with a pea under her body. Let's see what happens!"

As they ate breakfast the next day,
the queen asked if the girl had slept well.
"Actually, no!" yawned the girl.
"It's so strange. My bed was big and
squishy, but I could feel something
digging in to me."

"I knew it!" smiled the queen. "You are a true princess!" And so the prince had finally found someone to marry. Now the couple sleep well every night, and wake up happy each morning together.

The Princess and the Caterpillar

Princess Briar lived in a wonderful fairy kingdom. She was friends with all the animals and creatures that lived there. Her special favourite was a spider called Webster, who lived right outside Princess Briar's home.

One morning, Webster called out to her. "Princess Briar! Go quickly, and find a leaf. I have a job for you to do." Briar flew off to find a leaf and then hovered next to Webster to find out more.

Princess Briar followed her instructions. She hunted under the flowers and found a furry brown caterpillar that Webster had seen hiding there. "Come with me!" she squealed happily, and carried it away on her leaf.

She flew back home to find her mother, the Queen of the Fairies. "Look, Mama!" she shouted. "We must look after this caterpillar so that the birds don't eat it." Her mother was happy that her daughter wanted to help.

Every day, Princess Briar met
with Webster to tell him how her
caterpillar was doing. One day,
she had something odd to report.
"It has turned into a hard,
brown lump!" she said.

Webster told her not to worry, just to wait and watch. Sure enough, after a few days, the brown lump began to move. Princess Briar screamed with happiness when a beautiful butterfly crawled out!

As the butterfly tested its wings,
Princess Briar had a sudden thought.
Now she would no longer have
a caterpillar to care for.
"I'm going to miss you so much!"
she sobbed. "Don't worry,"
whispered the butterfly.

"I will bring my friends to see you!
And I know that there is another
caterpillar just over there, that needs your
help like I did." Sure enough, Briar soon
found a new furry friend, and had lots
of colourful, fluttery visitors, too!

Sleeping Beauty

The king and queen of a faraway land had always wanted a child. They waited many years until finally they were blessed with a daughter. They felt so lucky, and held a huge party to celebrate.

Everyone they could think of was
invited, and turned up with presents
for the baby. The only person left off
the guest list was the evil fairy,
Carabosse. As you can imagine,
she was very cross indeed.

Carabosse flew up to the princess and cast a spell. "Here is my present…on your sixteenth birthday you will prick your finger and die! Heh heh heh heh!" The other guests all gasped and wept.

Then the Fairy Rose spoke. "I still have a gift to give." She waved her wand. "My magic is not strong enough to undo the wicked spell. But the princess will not die. She will only sleep for a hundred years."

The king ordered that every sharp item should be taken away. The princess grew up happily, safe from any harm, until her sixteenth birthday.

Disguised as an old woman, Carabosse tricked the princess into pricking her finger.

The princess swooned and fell, and the king was called at once. He laid his daughter in her bed, and then fell asleep close by. The whole palace was under the spell, and everyone in it slept soundly.

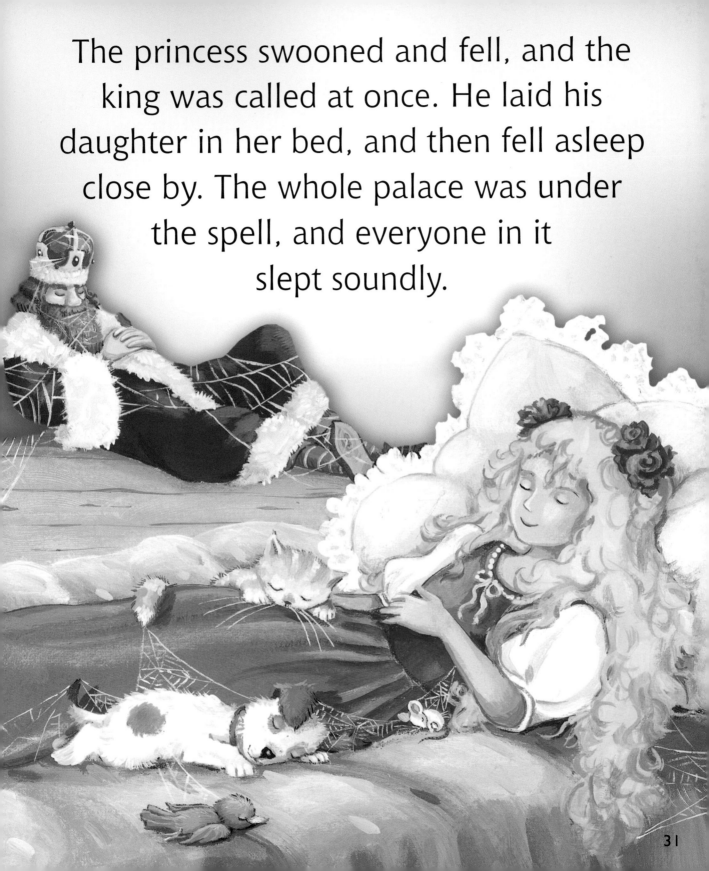

The people slept their enchanted sleep for a hundred years. A thick layer of thorns grew around the palace. One day, a young prince rode past. He saw the hidden palace and chopped his way to it with his sword.

Nervously, he rode inside. The silence was spooky. The prince searched through the rooms and found the sleeping princess. He kissed her hand and she opened her eyes. She told him what had happened and was so happy he had broken the spell!

Princess Rebecca
to the Rescue

Princess Rebecca was bored. It was a sunny day but she had no one to play with. She wished she had a brother or sister to cheer her up. The sad princess lay next to the royal lake and watched the swans glide past.

She rolled on the grass and watched a dragonfly hovering close by. Then she looked more closely. That wasn't a dragonfly – it was a tiny fairy in a pink dress, waving her wand! Princess Rebecca gasped.

The little pink fairy hovered
next to Princess Rebecca and
spoke to her. "I came as soon as
I heard your wish!" she said.
"But first, I need your help.
Are you feeling brave?"
Rebecca nodded.

"You must row to the island in the middle of the lake, and find the smallest swan of them all. Take the swan back to your palace and give it a home, and you will have a big surprise."

"But why?" asked Princess Rebecca. The fairy explained. The bird was actually a girl called Abigail who had been changed into a swan. A wicked wizard had cast a spell on her, and only a princess could undo the magic.

Princess Rebecca was so excited.
What an adventure! She ran down to
the boathouse to find her little rowing
boat. "Be careful!"
shouted the fairy,
as Rebecca raced
through the
reeds and
mud on the
banks of the
lake.

Carefully, she rowed her
boat to the island and looked
around. Hiding in some rushes
was a tiny swan with unusual
blue eyes. Rebecca gently
scooped it up and carried it
to her boat.

Back in the palace, the Princess filled her royal tub and lifted the swan into the water. With a flash, the swan was replaced by a smiling girl. The girls hugged each other. Now Rebecca wasn't alone any more!

The Little Mermaid

Deep at the bottom of the ocean,
a mermaid lived in a wonderful
underwater palace. Her father was
the Sea King and the mermaid was
the youngest of his
daughters.
Each daughter had
a special gift, and
her gift was a
beautiful singing
voice.

On her sixteenth birthday, the Little Mermaid was allowed to swim to the surface and look at the world above. It all looked so amazing! It made the Little Mermaid cry to think that she would never be able to leave the ocean.

Every night, the Little Mermaid
gazed at the stars and the ships.
One night, she stayed up for
hours, following a handsome
prince on a passing boat. She
watched him as he stared across
the ocean, although he did not
see her hiding in the foam.

Suddenly, the waves grew
large and thunder and lightning
ripped through the sky. The ship was
thrown high in the air, and the Prince
fell overboard. As quick as a flash,
the Little Mermaid swam to his side
and saved him from drowning.

Now the Little Mermaid wanted to leave the ocean more than ever. Her only way out was to buy a potion from the wicked sea witch. The old hag could give her legs instead of a tail, but at a high price.

The witch would take her beautiful voice so she could no longer talk or sing. Every step would feel like sharp knives were stabbing her. And if her beloved prince married someone else, the mermaid would be cast back to the sea.

As the mermaid swam to shore, her tail disappeared. She dragged herself out of the ocean and tried to walk. Ouch! It hurt so much that she fell down on the sand. That's when her prince appeared on the beach.

The prince couldn't understand why this lovely girl couldn't talk or walk. He knew she needed help, so he carried her gently home and looked after her. She spent many happy months in the prince's palace.

The mermaid hoped that the prince would begin to love her, and make all her pain worthwhile. But one day, he told her that he must marry someone else. The mermaid cried as she watched his wedding.

Her sisters called to her.
"Take this enchanted dagger and
kill the prince. Then you can return to
the sea with us!" But the mermaid couldn't
do it. She threw the dagger away, and was
swept up in the clouds for ever more.

A Real Princess

Ellie worked at the palace, looking after the King, the Queen and the Prince. She made their beds, cleaned their clothes, and polished their silver and gold. They never saw her, for she was careful to stay out of their way.

Each lunchtime Ellie went outside to eat her sandwich and talk to the royal horses. The horses nuzzled up to her whilst she made a fuss of them.
"I wish I was a princess with a pony of my own!" she would whisper.

When Ellie got home at night, she started work again. She had to look after her father, who was old and poorly. One night, as she cleaned the kitchen, she saw something sparkling underneath the cooker. It was a shiny diamond ring!

Ellie slipped the ring on her finger. She was so tired that she had to go to bed. By the morning she had forgotten all about it. She went to work at the palace and started work in the stables.

As Ellie put new straw on the ground, she heard the voice of the Prince. There was nowhere for her to hide! "Don't worry," said the Prince. "I was going to ask for your help. Please will you ride my horse today, as I'm too busy?"

Ellie was delighted. She finished her work quickly, and then climbed on the horse's back. "I wish we could ride far away to a land where I was a princess!" she sighed. Suddenly, her diamond ring flashed, and the horse galloped off at top speed.

After a while, the horse stopped galloping. Ellie was amazed to see a unicorn standing in front of her. "Welcome to your kingdom, Princess Elizabeth!" it said. "Your wish has come true!"

The unicorn spoke again.
"Your diamond ring will give
you two more wishes. What will
they be?" Princess Elizabeth wished
to have her darling father with her,
and a kind Prince to marry. And
guess which Prince appeared?

Rapunzel

Once upon a time, a poor father tried to steal some vegetables so that his children wouldn't starve. The vegetables belonged to a wicked witch, who punished the man by taking away his eldest daughter, Rapunzel.

The witch kept Rapunzel locked in a tall tower. The girl could not escape, for the tower had no door, and just a single window high up by the roof. She could only sing with the birds, and wait for the witch to visit.

Every day, the witch brought food to the tower. She stood at the bottom and cried out, "Rapunzel, Rapunzel, let down your hair!" The girl's hair was so long it reached the ground, and the witch could climb it like a ladder.

One day,
a prince heard
Rapunzel
singing and
stopped to
listen. He hid
when the witch
arrived, and
watched as she
called to the
girl and then
climbed up to
reach her.
How amazing!

The prince waited for the witch to leave, and then called out to Rapunzel. She was shocked to see a stranger appear in the tower! The two of them talked and laughed, and the prince promised to visit again.

True to his word, he came every day to keep Rapunzel company, and soon they were very much in love. Then one day, the witch found out their secret.

The witch hid in the tower and waited for the prince to call. As he climbed up Rapunzel's long hair, the witch chopped it off! The prince tumbled into the enchanted thorns below.

The witch was furious with Rapunzel, and led her deep into the forest. Left all alone, Rapunzel wept. Her tears dissolved all the thorns around, and there stood the prince. Now they live happily together on the ground floor of his castle!

Cinderella

Poor Cinderella lived a hard life.
Her mother had died, and her father
had married again. His new wife was
mean, with two wicked daughters.
They made Cinderella work very hard,
keeping the house clean and
looking after them all.

Cinderella's stepsisters had expensive dresses and lots of jewels. Cinderella had no nice clothes at all. She wore rags and no shoes. At night, she slept in the kitchen, curled up on the floor in front of the fire.

The nasty sisters were
going to a ball at the royal
palace. They were very
excited, as the Prince was
looking for a wife.
Cinderella wasn't
invited, but she had to
help the sisters get ready.
They wanted to look their
very best for the Prince.

After her stepsisters had
gone, Cinderella carried on
with her cleaning, washing
and cooking. Tears fell from
her eyes into the cooking
pot as she wished she could
go to the ball, too.

"I can make your wish come true!" said a singsong voice from the corner of the room. Cinderella gasped. There was a fairy, waving her wand! With one magic spell, the fairy changed Cinderella's rags into a beautiful ball dress.

The fairy took Cinderella outside and waved her wand again. Four mice running around the yard magically became majestic white horses. An old pumpkin turned into a fine coach fit for a princess. Cinderella gasped and clapped her hands.

"Go to the ball, and have a lovely time!" said the fairy. "But remember one thing. You must leave before midnight, when the magic ends, or the Prince will see who you really are." Cinderella thanked the fairy, and rode off in the magnificent coach.

Everyone gasped when Cinderella entered the ballroom. Nobody knew who she was, not even her stepsisters! The Prince danced with her all night. He didn't even look at anybody else. Cinderella wished the night could last forever.

At midnight, the clock began to strike
twelve. Cinderella gasped. "I have to go!"
she cried, and ran out of the palace.
The Prince ran after her, but she had gone.
All that he found was a single glass shoe.

The Prince took the glass shoe to hundreds of houses, trying to find the beautiful girl who had worn it. The mean stepsisters tried to squeeze into it, but their feet were too huge. Then the Prince saw Cinderella hiding in a corner.